EAT YOUR VEGETABLES!

HEALTHY EATING HABITS

Mary Elizabeth
Salzmann

Consulting Editor,
Diane Craig,
M.A./ Reading Specialist

Sandcastle

An Imprint of Abdo Publishing
www.abdopublishing.com

www.abdopublishing.com

Published by Abdo Publishing, a division of ABDO, PO Box 398166, Minneapolis, Minnesota 55439.
Copyright © 2015 by Abdo Consulting Group, Inc. International copyrights reserved in all countries. No part
of this book may be reproduced in any form without written permission from the publisher. SandCastle™ is a
trademark and logo of Abdo Publishing.

Printed in the United States of America, North Mankato, Minnesota
102014
012015

**THIS BOOK CONTAINS
RECYCLED MATERIALS**

Editor: Alex Kuskowski
Content Developer: Nancy Tuminelly
Cover and Interior Design: Colleen Dolphin, Mighty Media, Inc.
Photo Credits: Shutterstock

Library of Congress Cataloging-in-Publication Data

Salzmann, Mary Elizabeth, 1968- author.

 Eat your vegetables! : healthy eating habits / Mary Elizabeth Salzmann.

   pages cm. -- (Healthy habits)

 ISBN 978-1-62403-529-6 (alk. paper)

1. Nutrition--Juvenile literature. 2. Dietetics--Juvenile literature. 3. Health--Juvenile literature. I. Title. II. Series:
Salzmann, Mary Elizabeth, 1968- Healthy habits.

 TX355.S235 2015

 613.2083--dc23

                    2014023593

SandCastle™ Level: Transitional

SandCastle™ books are created by a team of professional educators, reading specialists, and content developers around
five essential components—phonemic awareness, phonics, vocabulary, text comprehension, and fluency—to assist young
readers as they develop reading skills and strategies and increase their general knowledge. All books are written, reviewed,
and leveled for guided reading, early reading intervention, and Accelerated Reader® programs for use in shared, guided, and
independent reading and writing activities to support a balanced approach to literacy instruction. The SandCastle™ series
has four levels that correspond to early literacy development. The levels are provided to help teachers and parents select
appropriate books for young readers.

EMERGING · BEGINNING · **TRANSITIONAL** · FLUENT

CONTENTS

WHAT IS A HEALTHY HABIT?

Eating right is
a healthy **habit**.

MyPlate can help you eat right.

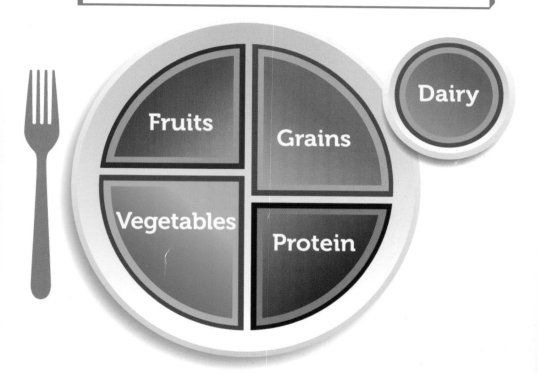

ChooseMyPlate.gov

It shows the five food groups. Eat foods from each group every day.

9

Matt and Olivia like vegetables.
They eat **salad** with dinner.

Cherries are Carlo's **favorite** fruit. He eats some for a snack.

Cereal is made from grain. Erin and her dad eat cereal for breakfast.

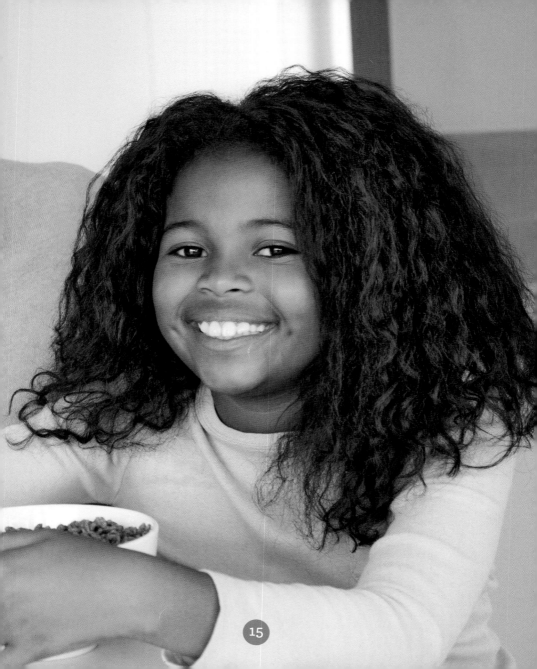

Protein comes from meat, nuts, **beans**, and eggs. Eli eats a **hamburger** at a **picnic**.

Milk, cheese, and **yogurt** are in the dairy group. Amy likes to drink milk.

Sweets are not on MyPlate.
To be healthy, only eat
them sometimes.

What do you do
to eat right?

HEALTH QUIZ

1. Eating right is not a healthy **habit**.
   True or False?

2. MyPlate cannot help you eat right.
   True or False?

3. MyPlate shows the five food groups.
   True or False?

4. Carlo eats cherries for a snack.
   True or False?

5. Erin and her dad eat **cereal** for
   breakfast. True or False?

Answers: 1. False 2. False 3. True 4. True 5. True

23

GLOSSARY

bean – a seed or a pod that you can eat.

cereal – a breakfast food made from grain and eaten with milk.

favorite – someone or something that you like best.

habit – a behavior done so often that it becomes automatic.

hamburger – a sandwich that has a cooked patty of ground beef on a round bun.

picnic – a meal eaten outdoors, often while sitting on the ground.

protein – a substance needed for good health, found naturally in meat, eggs, beans, and nuts.

salad – a mixture of raw vegetables usually served with a dressing.

yogurt – a food made with milk and often mixed with fruit.